TATE THE GREAT

JERYL CHRISTMAS

Illustrated by Paul Tirol

This Book Belongs To

_____

This book is dedicated to my great nephew Tate, who likes to think outside the box and never allows his imagination to waver.

There once was a boy named Tate
whose dream was to be first mate
on a big sailing ship
with a sword on his hip
seeing sights on a seafaring trip.

The first thing he spied
was a porpoise that was tied
to the bow of the ship
down below.
It said it would lead
like a sleek majestic steed.
Awesome sights and unknown
things it would show.

So off Tate did go
with his sailing ship in tow
to embark on this
fanciful trip,
to grant his special wish
just to see all the fish
and try hard just to stay
aboard the ship.

The clown fish, the eels,
the octopus, and seals
were all such a sight
to behold
that on a sudden whim
Tate jumped in so he could swim
with all the sea life, even though
the sea was cold.

A dolphin swimming by
looked at Tate and told him, "Hi."
Then he said to grab
his fin for a hold.
Tate grabbed it like he should,
making sure his grip was good.
Underwater he did just
as he was told.

The dolphin took him miles,
but tired "Tatey" was all smiles
as they glided on and even
surfed a wave.
Swimmers looking on
stared in awe at this unknown
of a dolphin and a boy
who was so brave.

Then a lobster captured Tate,
and he worried for his fate.
Was it going to be a friend or
fearsome foe?
She said she needed aid
for the eggs that she had laid
and to a dark and scary place
he'd have to go.

Her eggs were swept away
by a current late that day
and were trapped inside a cave
on rocky ground.
She needed Tate to help
put them back into the kelp
so they could hatch into the sea
where they were bound.

A turtle helped him rise
to the wide and open skies.
Tate took in a long and
needed breath of air.
He abandoned his daydreaming,
where his thinking it was seeming
to be lost in wonderland
without a care.

But Tate discovered this—
if you want some frequent bliss,
imagination is a very
useful tool.
It can take you far away
in your mind on any day.
It can really be adventurous
and cool.

So be creative in your thinking
when you feel your mind is sinking.
Remember that you're
clever as a fox.
Don't let life fence you in.
Just imagine and begin
to expand your mind and think
outside the box.

THE END

www.ingramcontent.com/pod-product-compliance
Lightning Source LLC
Chambersburg PA
CBHW041009170626
46815CB00002B/224